Girls' Day

March 3 in Japan is Girls' Day, called *Hina Matsuri*, the Doll Festival. Parents display *hina* dolls in their homes to wish their daughters good health and happiness.

Boys' Day

May 5 is *Tango no Sekku*, the Boys' Festival. On this day parents fly or hang carp kites, a symbol of courage and strength, to celebrate their sons.

YOKO'S Show-and-Tell

ROSEMARY WELLS

Disney · Hyperion Books

NEW YORK

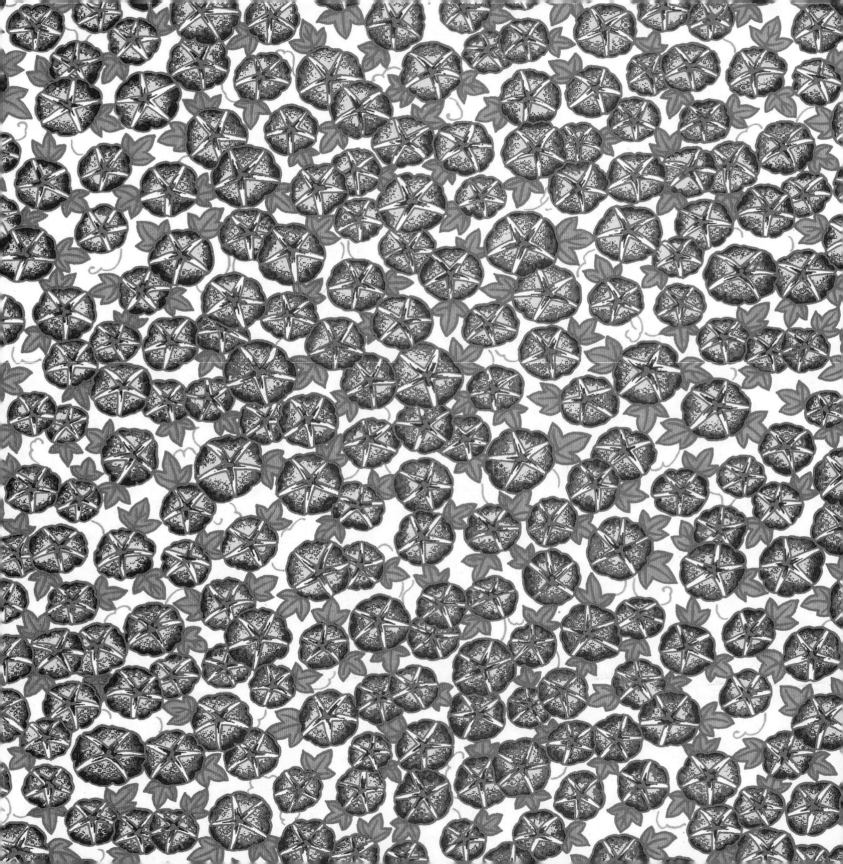

One afternoon, when the wind blew and the snow flew,
the mailman knocked on the door.
He had a package for Yoko.
It had come all the way from Japan.

Yoko opened the package carefully.
Inside was a little doll in a kimono.

こんにちは

My name is Miki.
Long ago I belonged to your Mama,
before that to your obaasan
and great obaasan.
Please sit me on my red carpet
steps and bring me candy
until Girls' day!
Obaasan and Ojiisan
will visit soon after!

愛

There was a note from Yoko's *obaasan* and *ojiisan*,
her granny and grandpa in Japan.

Yoko's mama helped Yoko arrange the red carpet
for Miki. Yoko placed Miki in the window and
brought her candy each morning.
By evening, the candy was gone.

At last the morning of Girls' Day came, March 3.
Yoko brought Miki a platter of peach-blossom cakes
that her mama had made in honor of the celebration.

"At my school they don't know about Girls' Day,"
said Yoko. "I will take Miki to school for show-and-tell!"
"Miki is too delicate to take to school," said Yoko's mama.

"Please, please, please, Mama!" said Yoko.

Yoko's mama shook her head.

In her Big No voice she told Yoko,

"We don't trouble trouble, or trouble will trouble us!"

But Yoko was too excited about Girls' Day.

"Everyone in my class will love you!" she said to Miki.

"I will bring you right home, and Mama will never know!"

On the school bus, the Franks saw Miki
peeking out of Yoko's coat.
"What's that, Yoko?" asked Frank.
"You'll see in show-and-tell," said Yoko.

"I want to see now!" Frank grabbed Miki from Yoko.
He tossed Miki all the way down the aisle of the
school bus.

"No!" said Yoko. "Please! No!"
"Hey! This is fun!" said the other Frank.
Back and forth Miki went.

At last Miki bounced off the ceiling
and landed in a mud puddle on the bus floor.

"We are going to be in so much trouble with
Mrs. Jenkins, it's not even funny!" said the Franks.

In school, Mrs. Jenkins asked, "Do you have a
show-and-tell surprise for us today, Yoko?"
Yoko could not answer.

Yoko could not do her singing or drawing.
She would not eat lunch.
Mrs. Jenkins called Yoko's mama.

Yoko's mama drove Yoko home from school.
"Tea and sweet-bean candy will make you feel better,
my little lotus flower," said Yoko's mama.

But nothing helped.

"I'll get Miki!" said Yoko's mama.

"She'll make you smile!"

"No!" said Yoko.

Yoko brought out poor ruined Miki.
"Do you still love me?" Yoko asked her mama.

Yoko's mama whispered, "You have made a bad mistake, my little lotus flower, but I love you just as much as ever!"

"We will take Miki to the emergency room of
Dr. Kiroshura's doll hospital," said Yoko's mama.

"What a terrible accident!" said Dr. Kiroshura.
"Miki will have to go into surgery right away!"

All week long Yoko went to the doll hospital during visiting hours. Yoko brought red bean candy and sat next to Miki's bed.

Dr. Kiroshura mended Miki's arms. He repaired the crack in her face and applied a new nose. Miki's lips were repainted so smoothly and neatly, you could see no scars at all.

Yoko's mama sewed a brand-new kimono of flowered silk.

Yoko made Miki a pair of new white cotton socks.

"Miki may go home tomorrow," said Dr. Kiroshura.

Miki was all ready for Obaasan and Ojiisan's springtime visit from Japan.

Obaasan admired Miki's new kimono.
"She is so beautiful. And not one scratch after all
these years!" she said.

"Who is that outside, scrubbing the steps, raking all the peach blossoms, and pulling up the weeds?" asked Ojiisan.

With thanks to Kathie S.

All rights reserved. Published by Disney • Hyperion Books, an imprint of Disney Book Group.
No part of this book may be reproduced or transmitted in any form or by any means,
electronic or mechanical, including photocopying, recording, or by any information storage and
retrieval system, without written permission from the publisher.
For information address Disney • Hyperion Books, 114 Fifth Avenue,
New York, New York 10011-5690.
Printed in Singapore
First Edition
1 3 5 7 9 10 8 6 4 2
F850-6835-5-10319
Reinforced binding
Library of Congress Cataloging-in-Publication Data on file.
ISBN 978-1-4231-1955-5
Visit www.hyperionbooksforchildren.com
Japanese calligraphy by Masako Inkyo